MURDER AT THE MIDLAND HOTEL

"Murder on the Dance Floor"

Novella No.1

By A. D. Padgett

Dedicated to

STS

Published by

Murder On The Dance Floor

First Published 2010

Copyright A. D. Padgett 2010

ISBN 978-0-9561587-5-8

DISCLAIMER: The characters in this book are purely fictitious and any resemblance to real persons is purely coincidental.

MURDER AT THE MIDLAND HOTEL

∽THE CALL∾

Rachel Foxe is in her mid 40's. She lives in London, Islington, near the Angel Tube Station. Her top floor flat in Bromfield Street overlooks the Business Design Centre. She has a PhD in sociology but, to avoid staying an academic all her life, she became an investigative journalist, a private investigator and, when she gets the chance, a dancer. She has red hair and is a passionate dancer, and a fiery detective.

She is answering a phone call whilst staring from her window.

A very pleasant lady, by the name of Gwen Johnson, wants her to investigate into the whereabouts of a chap called Cedric, her missing husband. He has been missing for 10 years and she wants to see him to get his agreement in a divorce.

It's a matter of principle for her that he signs the papers. She probably still loves him, thought Rachel, after all this time. Her heart went out to her.

Anyway, Gwen has had a tip-off from Professor Bill Marsh, her cousin once removed, who believes that Cedric will be at the Midland Hotel, Morecambe, for a dinner dance. Gwen suspected that her husband was somewhere in the North West area so things are beginning to fall into place. The Professor knows Cedric as Thomas and has got to know him over the last couple of years but hadn't put two and two together until now. Too busy with his research probably. That and the fact that the professor had never met Cedric. He had seen photographs of him but Cedric's appearance has changed if he is Thomas. His dark hair has become grey and his clean shaven face has become bearded.

Gwen would like to set a little trap for old Cedric at the Midland dinner dance and has come to Rachel because her website says that she is "a private detective, with a flair for dance."

"This will interest you as Cedric used to teach a bit of Swing. So you might even end up dancing with him. You will be the guest of the Professor. We've arranged for you all to be on the same table and there you can watch Cedric, and I'm sure it is Cedric from the photographs the Professor has sent me. But I want you to find out all you can before you put it to him that he is my husband. I want to see what he claims."

"Well I'm always happy to take a case, especially one where there is dancing and a party involved."

"Yes, we have a room for you in the hotel, but promise not to drink. There will be plenty of champagne flowing if I know these events."

"No. I never drink at work or drink and dance for that matter."

"Yes, but this is a very serious matter. And just a word of warning, I think he has got into bad company since I knew him, so please look after yourself, and please don't let the Professor get too involved."

Rachel turns to Troubles, her white cat with a black and grey striped tail. He is a moggy, not a pedigree. He is a big, stocky, teddy bear cat. Blind in one eye. A rescue cat. She cuddles him and begins to sing.

"Pack up your "Troubles" in your old kitty bag and smile, girl, smile."

✑THE ARRIVAL✒

The day of the dance Rachel Foxe had driven up the M6 in her classic white British MG Midget sports car. The autumn air was too cold to have the roof down but when she got near the seaside resort of Morecambe, Lancashire, on the North West coast of England, she had stopped to lower the roof. Now she basks in the rays and the fresh air.

Her sunglasses sit on the bridge of her nose and her hair is covered by a shawl. She is elegant and sophisticated with a bone structure to match. It comes as a package.

There is a tartan blanket over the cat basket in the passenger seat. She is bringing her "Troubles" with her.

As she drives along the promenade she ignores the decadence of the seaside hotels to her left, deserted since holidaymakers stopped going on British seaside holidays, preferring cheap flights to resorts with guaranteed Mediterranean sunshine. She ignores the amusement arcades, the buckets and spades, the rubber rings, the sticks of rock and the ice cream parlours. Instead she concentrates on the road ahead and glances at the splendour of the Lake District mountains to her right. Beautiful, stunning views of Morecambe bay. Maybe seaside chic is back in style.

"Oh," she remarks with surprise as she passes one of Morecambe's most famous landmarks, a statue commemorating the comedian Eric Morecambe, the town's most famous son. The statue is silhouetted on the skyline and surrounded with tourists imitating his one legged stance. She starts to hum "Bring me sunshine" to herself, smiling as she drives.

Ahead of her the Midland Hotel, a Grade 2* listed building, comes into view. It's white exterior gleaming in the sun. A sleek, unique modernist masterpiece. An internationally renowned Art-Deco classic, a monument to 1930's style. "How strange," she thought, "that a hotel in the north should be called "The Midland"."

On her left she passes a large red sandstone structure, another of Morecambe's landmark buildings. Partially renovated, a standing sign outside boasted the name The Winter Gardens. Clearly this was once a grand theatre and ballroom where famous comedians and big bands would have performed. But now it is flanked by amusement arcades and pound shops.

She returns to her present excitement. She is approaching <u>the</u> place to be in Morecambe. Located centrally on the promenade, restored, like back in the 1930's, in all its glory, the Midland Hotel.

The building resembles an old cinema or a Brighton mansion, or a swimming pool, a lido. These are the only other art deco buildings Rachel is familiar with, although she would like to pretend she knows more. The design is almost like a liner, as ship in dock. Rachel can see its walls gracefully curving along the North West coast as she draws near.

The low white wall has two entrance openings, each flanked with spiralling concrete scrolls. The first is upon her in no time, so she chooses the second, indicating and pulling into a gap in the central reservation. She pulls off the main road and passes between the two stone columns, into the entrance. The huge car park is smooth to drive on and the Midget glides over the new tarmac surface. She avoids the BMW saloons, the black 4 x 4s and the expensive sports cars. None of them as classic as the Midget, she thinks, convincing herself that money cannot buy style.

Then her eyebrow rises at a 1930's style kit car. It is a red roadster and it has its hood down. "Nice touch," she thinks.

She parks up her small car next to a palm tree that stands incongruously in the centre of the tarmac sea. A living remnant from the building's earlier days. She puts on the steering lock.

Getting out of the car she removes her headscarf, turns down the collar on her raincoat and then pulls the car hood up, fixing it into place. She then gets her bags from the boot and finally opens the side door and lifts "Troubles", in his basket, from the seat.

Then she heads towards the iconic entrance tower. It stands, a cylinder, in the centre of the hotel. Three magnificent columns of window rise up it, culminating in two carved seahorses. They guard the entrance and break up the flat lines of the roof. The building instantly evokes a classic era and Rachel is transported to moving images of Fred Estaire and Ginger Rogers, dancing in 1930's black and white movies.

She walks up the stairs, towards the smoked glass doors, flanked by sea green lettering spelling "MIDLAND" on one side and "HOTEL" on the other.

The doors open and her eyes adjust to the light levels of the room beyond.

⇜ENTRANCE LOBBY⇝

As Rachel enters the hotel the sweet smell of lilies hits her. She takes it in as she looks around. 1930's jazz music is playing.

She walks forward and sees a large lobby, split into two sides, but does not notice the tower rising three floors above her.

On the right sit guests, chatting, in low red leather armchairs, a table of lilies in their midst. They are all on a large round carpet, with wave-like patterns, that is placed there for both comfort and effect.

On the left is a long black reception desk. A thin young man sits at the desk. An older man stands beside him. Both wear black shirts. Behind them Rachel recognises the famous Eric Gill carved relief.

She approaches the desk, ready for checking in. The men seem to be in the middle of a telephone booking so she waits patiently, admiring the white limestone relief. It is very flat and the figures are cut only in outline, incised with details, of faces, arms and folds of skirts, as if they had been drawn on. It was strangely reminiscent of the Egyptian or Babylonian carvings she had seen at the British Museum, only it was definitely less sculptural.

She picks up an information sheet from the desk and reads.

"The 16ft by 10ft bas-relief is named "Odysseus welcomed from the sea by Nausicaa." It was carved in situ from Portland stone and was completed in 1933, just after Eric Gill's celebrated "Prospero and Ariel" relief, which stands on the front of BBC Broadcasting House. Nausicaa is beside a tree attended by three semi-naked maids. One carries a bowl of fruit, the second a jug and cup and the third a robe. She helps Odysseus from the water."

Her gaze returns to the relief and she notices an inscription running along the bottom.

"What does that say?" asks Rachel as she careens over the desk, peering.

"THERE IS GOOD HOPE THAT THOU MAYEST SEE THY FRIENDS." From Homer's Odysseus," replies the thin, young receptionist.

"Well, is there good hope that thou mayest book me in and give me my keys?"

"As you have referenced a famous poem then I will," smiles the young man. "Name please."

"Rachel Foxe."

The older man beside him interrupts. "I'm Sebastian Farquhar, the Assistant Manager." He looks at the computer screen. "Your room is on the second floor. I'll show you where it is. I'm going that way anyway." The man came across as someone who liked asserting control. Delegating tasks that he didn't want to do, reserving the "interesting" jobs for himself. "Strange that I should have that impression," thinks Rachel.

She moves back under the entrance area and now notices the tower. Looking directly upwards she enjoys the way the spiral staircase winds around, like the shell of a sea snail.

In the middle of the ceiling, at the top of the circular staircase, is a medallion, about 10 feet in diameter. It is coloured blue, green, yellow and shades of red brown. She makes out a crowned figure, presumably Neptune, God of the sea, sitting on a throne, with two mermaids behind him, as another figure emerges from the sea holding a golden horn.

"It was carved by Eric Gill and painted by his son-in-law. And before you ask, the inscription says –AND HEAR OLD TRITON BLOW HIS WREATHED HORN, words from an 1807 Wordsworth sonnet." The assistant manager smiles as he takes one of her bags. But his manner makes her unsure whether to be appreciative, or not.

They head up, on a plush red carpet. To their right are the long windows she had seen from outside. She holds the steel hand-rail, its design echoing the rectangles of the window frames.

At the first floor level is a full length, black and white, photographic "mural" of the 1930's hotel. On it are super-imposed colour photographs of chairs and sculptures.

"The hotel is a very elegant design."

"And you are a very elegant lady."

He smiles as they walk the length of the photograph. "How indiscrete," thinks Rachel as she considers whether Sebastian's features are chiselled or just weaselled. She will be glad to get to her room.

They continue to rise. And at the second floor level is another photographic mural, the same. Passing this long photograph they step up into a narrow corridor.

☙☠☜

~THE ROOM~

The red carpet continues to stretch in a gentle curve to the far end of the building. They stop at a white door, half way along the coffee coloured walls. The assistant manager puts down her bag and opens the door into a chocolate coloured room with a coffee carpet.

The first thing Rachel does is go to the window to admire the magnificent view. She can see right across the bay to the Lake District hills. "It's beautiful," she says, "though it looks like rain clouds are closing in." She pauses. "Truly beautiful."

The assistant manager is about to reply, but stops himself.

There are two beds, both with crisp white sheets and bright red cushions, and she puts "Troubles" onto one of them.

The assistant manager puts her bag by the other bed and turns on the light. "Your shower is just around the corner..."

Rachel turns to face him. "Thank you. That's fine, I'll find everything."

He cocks his head and raises an eyebrow. "I hope you enjoy your stay with us and if there is anything you need then don't hesitate to ask."

As he leaves, Rachel sees a vertical white radiator and a flat, white, semi-abstract tree sculpture on the wall, both in the corner next to the closing door. "Strange but stylish," she muses, then crouches down to stare at Troubles. "Isn't it exciting staying here!" She lifts him from his basket and cuddles him, remembering that she has work to do.

Troubles sits watching as she takes off her black Mac and begins to unpack.

When everything is in order she straightens her white shirt and black waistcoat, to get comfortable, and then lays back onto the bed. She turns over and looks at Troubles, smiling.

She notices a hotel brochure, finds her glasses and begins to read to Troubles.

"The London, Midland and Scottish Railway Company selected the architect Oliver Hill to build a modern structure on the site of an existing Victorian Hotel building and the Midland was completed in 1932." She stops reading. "Ah that's why it is called the Midland, after the railway company," then continues. "The Midland quickly attracted socialites, wealthy mill-owners and businessmen from across the north of England and became the place to stay. But its heyday came to an abrupt end with the declaration of war in 1939."

"After the war, the building was in a bad state of repair and a large amount of money had to be spent to renovate the building. The Midland was re-opened in 1948. The 1950s showed another period of popularity but trade slowed by the 1970s. And although a glass sun-lounge (running the length of the seaward side of the hotel) was added in the late 1970's the business did not improve and by the late 1980's the hotel was very run down."

"In 2003 the hotel was purchased by the Manchester based development company Urban Splash. They spent two years preparing plans and acquiring £7.2 million of funding to finance the project. Essential repair work to the fabric of the building began in 2005. The restoration took three years to complete and the hotel re-opened in June 2008."

It begins to rain.

"Urban Splash have achieved a balance between preservation and the needs of a modern hotel. The ground floor has been restored as closely as possible to the original but the bedrooms have been brought up to a luxury standard. The old sun lounge has been replaced by a lighter, glazed structure and six luxury suites have been added on to the roof of the hotel. Now at the hotel there are 44 boutique rooms, a sea view Restaurant and Rotunda café (serving cocktails and meals) plus an on site Spa..."

Rachel is tired from her drive. She drops the brochure. The fatigue from the journey settles in as she and Troubles settle in.

Both fall asleep.

❧THE RAVILIOUS BAR❧

It is late afternoon and Rachel is late for her appointment to meet the Professor.

She picks up Troubles and heads down the corridor, then remembers she has forgotten her lip gloss. She quickly goes back, puts Troubles on the bed and heads into the bathroom to get it. When she comes back the cat is gone.

She looks under the bed and then nips out of the door.

"Troubles, where are you?"

She walks briskly down the corridor to the top of the stairs and sees him, a large ball of white, sitting on the lobby floor, on a mosaic sea horse.

"There you are." She nips down the stairs and picks him up. "Always up to mischief." And heads down to the rotunda café.

She passes through a red corridor, recessed with red leather booths, to a circular room at the north end of the hotel. A circular bar dominates the room and above the bar is a lamp shade made of what looks to be like upside down plastic cups. It is a giant stalactite that defies gravity, like a prop from a science fiction movie. She sits on a stool and places Troubles on another, then orders a latte from the bar man, who is dressed in the hotel uniform black.

She sips her latte, and decides that it is hot enough, then looks through the windows at the passing tourists and people of Morecambe. An elderly couple is walking their small Scottish terrier dog. A man passes on his bicycle, recklessly avoiding a young woman who pushes her pram, whilst pulling a toddler behind her. A group of youths in black shell-suits marches past, laughing and pushing each other as they go.

She sips her latte when an elderly man, with a young lady, approaches around the bar.

The man is medium height and has balding, grey hair. He is a dapper dresser, in an open blue shirt with a white boating jacket that has thick black pin stripes. He is slightly overweight but looks fit and has a very serious manner. The lady is beautiful and blonde. She looks casual and confident in her dark blue flared jeans and pale pink cashmere jumper.

"Hello, you must be Rachel. I'm Professor Bill Marsh and this is my daughter, Charlotte."

The man wears his title like it is natural, as if it was always there. He clearly enjoys being flamboyant and looking the part. But he takes more the role of a businessman than a dusty old academic. He is more a European or an American Professor, not so much an English one. Here is an international academic, a man who attends conferences in Geneva, Italy or America.

Rachel shakes his hand. "Hi. Pleasure to meet you."

"Sorry we're late," says Charlotte. "It's all my fault. I was teaching the Charleston, ready for tonight," she bends down. "Oh your cat is beautiful, what's his name?"

"Troubles. Even when I'm on holiday I can't leave my "Troubles" behind," she laughs.

"Can I stroke him?"

Rachel lifts Troubles up. "He's gorgeously cuddly but will only allow me to cuddle him."

Charlotte strokes his head as Troubles squeezes his eyes shut, pretending to suffer, but continuing to purr.

"He's a rescue cat, and is still slightly timid because of it. He's remarkably intuitive and has an unstinting sense of adventure, but that doesn't contradict his timidity, which is restricted to people, not situations."

Charlotte gives an understanding nod. "Did you come by train?" she asks.

"No, I came in the Midget."

"The Midget?"

"Oh, sorry, the car, an old British sports car."

"Sounds great fun. I've a red 1930's kit car."

"Yes, I saw it. It's beautiful."

The Professor interrupts their chatting. "So, Gwen has sent you to do some work for us."

"Yes, Mrs Johnson has commissioned me to carry out some business for her."

"And how exactly do you describe your line of business?"

"I'm an investigative journalist, but I also take on other work, you know, finding lost husbands and such."

"So you mean you are a private eye?"

'I prefer to call myself a private detective," says Rachel to the Professor, then turns to Charlotte, "with a flair for dance."

"So you could say you are a dancing detective?" laughs Charlotte.

Rachel raises an eyebrow. "Yes, I rather like that."

Charlotte leans forward. "Do you read murder mysteries?"

"No, I never touch the things," says Rachel with a cheeky sparkle in her eye.

Charlotte smiles. "Did you know "Double Sin", an episode of Agatha Christie's "Poirot" was filmed right here. This was known as the Ravilious Bar, because its interior was painted by Eric Ravilious, a well-known artist at the time. But his mural of a fantasy seaside and firework display began to peel off almost immediately and the TV crew had to re-paint it for filming. They made it into a fabulous tea room. But I rather like this new look."

The Professor is about to speak but Charlotte continues. "I've often thought of writing a murder mystery? I think I have a book in me..."

"Sounds positively painful," interrupts the Professor. "Sorry, Charlotte, I didn't mean that. We just need to talk business at the moment." He opens a wallet and takes out some photographs. "I suspect that Thomas Smythe may be Gwen's husband, Cedric. Here, take these photos."

"Thanks, Gwen has already e-mailed them to me."

"He's a dead-ringer," continues the Professor, "but the matter needs treating with utmost discretion. I don't want my cousin to find out more than she needs to. Thomas is married to Suzie, and if he is married to someone else, then that makes him a bigamist. What's more is that he's involved in some pretty shady business dealings."

"And what makes you suspect that he is Gwen's husband?" asks Rachel.

"I'd already thought there was a similarity but what tipped it was when I found out that he was already married. He was sitting in one of those booths over there one night," the Professor points to some red leather alcoves, "and he'd had one cocktail too many. I overheard him on his mobile. He was telling his new wife, Suzie, that his old wife was getting wind of where he was and wanted a divorce, but he would rather see her dead than give her that pleasure. I was so disgusted to hear what he was saying that I confronted him, and asked him if he was married to Gwen. He got a bit shirty, almost violent, about my listening in to his conversation, so I grabbed my coat and left. I went downstairs to the toilets. I sat wondering what to do when I heard Thomas and," the Professor begins to whisper, "Sebastian Farquhar, the assistant manager of the Midland, coming down the stairs, talking."

"Oh yes, that was the man who showed me to my room," says Rachel.

"Yes, he won't be working here much longer though. The hotel manager has had concerns about him for a while.

The manager just wants to watch what's happening for the minute though. And he's away on holiday at the moment so Farquhar has got the run of the place. Anyway, I wanted to know what they were up to, so I hid in the ladies' cubicles."

Rachel raises an eyebrow.

The Professor continues "They had been working on a plan to steal the Eric Gill relief. You know the one behind the reception desk?" Rachel nods. "It ranks as one of Eric Gill's best works and is valued at 2 million pounds. Anyway, I saw red and came out and confronted them, warning them not to plan any further or I would tell the police."

"But how could they walk off with a great stone relief, it's six tonnes?" asks Charlotte.

"Maybe they would send it for exhibition in London," says Rachel, "wait for its fame and its value to increase even further and then fake a hijack when it was in transit on its way back home."

The Professor smiles. "Very quick, you're a smart cookie."

"There's no out-foxing me," winks Rachel as Charlotte shakes her head in disbelief.

"Well, its been done before you know. There was one very famous incident at the hotel," says the Professor. "By the early 1990s, the Gill relief was worth more than the hotel. So after the hotel's late owner lent it to the Barbican, in London, for an exhibition, he never brought it back. The town councillors suspected that he had been trying to sell it, so they took him to court. They claimed that it was part of the listed building and not just 'fixtures and fittings' that the owner could sell. After seven years of legal wrangles, a court order denied the owner the right to sell it and ordered its return to the Midland. So the owner begrudgingly agreed to reinstate it to the walls of the Midland."

Rachel drinks her latte with Troubles on her lap as she listens intently.

"So "Odysseus" was boxed up in fourteen crates of several hundredweight and finally came 'home'. But even then it was just put in storage in the hotel's Sun Lounge. Then, in 1999, the owner died suddenly and, shortly after, the Council found that it was missing again. Eleven months later surveillance officers from the National Organised Crime Squad found it in the back of a van in West Yorkshire. After that it remained holed up in boxes in the Council's vaults until the new owner took over. So, you see, it's been done before and they want to do it again. The two of them told me they were just joking. I know they weren't but I haven't any evidence and I'd rather that Gwen didn't know about any of this."

"Problem is," says Charlotte, "how can we find out if Thomas is Auntie Gwen's long lost husband."

"I will be asking him questions at dinner and watching his reactions," says Rachel.

"Like a wily old "fox"?" asks the Professor.

"More of the wily and less of the old, I think," smiles Rachel.

"Well, you will have your work cut out tonight," says Charlotte. "You will have to be very subtle. There will be more vamps there than at Dracula's castle."

"Charlotte."

"Sorry father."

"Anyway, we'll go home to get changed. Then we'll meet you, with my fiancé, Barbara, and Charlotte's partner, Charles, in the lobby at 7pm, for Champagne reception. After the reception we will go to our table together."

"Splendid. I shall look forward to it. Do you live nearby?"

"Not far," says Charlotte, "in Lancaster, just near the University. We're staying here tonight, I just forgot some parts for my outfit, so we have to go back."

Rachel asks them where the toilets are. They point and then she finds a little white character, a bit like a Christmas tree, that symbolises "Ladies" and follows the curving stairway down.

It opens into a room with long, horizontal mirrors and sinks which flank an opening to the cubicles. 1930's music is being played and the vinyl floor is coloured a deep sea-green. Angular stripes, resembling waves, are on the wallpaper.

All is not what it seems. She touches the arm of one of the comfy looking white arm chairs. It is solid, moulded plastic. So she puts Troubles onto it and then she steps back, in shock, as the Professor enters the room from a door on the opposite side.

"Don't worry," he says holding up his hands as if gently pushing away her reaction, "this entrance area is unisex, the ladies and the gents wash hands together." Rachel raises her eyebrows. Now she understands how easily the Professor could have hidden.

"We'll see you tonight."

"Just wait here Troubles," reassures Rachel as she continues, feeling awkward, to the cubicles, where the ladies and the gents are separated only by a thin wall.

When Rachel returns up to the rotunda café the sun is beginning to set, so she sits outside to watch.

The flat roof of the cafe hangs over the curved café walls like the brim of a hat. The rectangular framed windows reflect the last minutes of the sun. This is classic art deco style. True seaside chic.

She sits on one of the curved black frame chairs. It is hard, and designed like a knotted rope, coiled onto upturned urns. She strokes Troubles and gazes from the patio area, past the steps that head down, in concentric circles, like ripples from a pool, leading to the promenade.

There had been a downpour whilst she was napping in her room and now the air is clear and clean. The grey, blue, black clouds have separated and are lit on their far side, warm like glowing embers, by the setting sun.

The globe lamps, on top of tall white posts, light up as the sun sets.

Behind the clouds the vivid blue sky fades into the last light of the horizon. The tide is out, running back to Neptune, leaving channels, and calm, still water pools in the ripples of sand, formed by the currents of his sea. The surface of the remnant water is alive with the reflection of a sky that is slowly dying, becoming cold, as the remnants of the sun disappear.

The bright white light of Jupiter becomes clear as the sky grows black. Then this planet, named after the highest Roman God, known as Zeus by the Greeks, slowly disappears behind thickening clouds.

All that is left is an orange glow of light cast upwards from Morecambe's street lamps.

Rachel shivers as she heads back to her room, past the reception lobby and up the spiral staircase.

As she steps into the corridor she catches the assistant manager and an elegant older lady. They quickly separate from an embrace. They stand, looking rather guilty, then pretend to be mid-conversation. "So it would be good to get your feedback from the evening in case we decide to do another one," he says.

"Yes, I'll see you this evening," she replies.

"He must think that women were made for him," thinks Rachel. "He's like a light and they are the moths. He's the kind of man who is always on the lookout, his eyes never resting in one place long enough to appreciate the full beauty of what he has. Constantly looking for the next treasure. Ohh, how unsavoury."

❧THE CHAMPAGNE RECEPTION❧

Rachel changes into a sparkly black dress, ready for the evening. It reaches almost to the floor and has no back to it, reaching down her spine to reveal her beautifully formed back. Leaving Troubles behind she heads down the corridor and steels herself before descending the staircase.

She makes no great effort but because she knows that people think she does she almost has a desire to be a little bit extra, to walk with a straighter than usual back, not to prove anything to herself, but just because people seem to expect it of her. She is happy not to be part of the crowd. She feels slightly different and wants to protect that difference, so she can remain just slightly outside.

She looks from high onto the lobby below. It is awash with the buzz of excited guests and diners. Then, feeling like a figure descending from the Greek heavens she heads down the staircase to the Champagne reception below.

She waits, avoiding being caught in the photograph of a couples posing at the foot of the staircase. Then she makes her way through the busy throng as camera flashes, of local press and friends, add to the glamour.

The staff serve champagne in flute stem glasses. They are dressed in authentic period uniform and guests are wearing 1920's and 1930's costumes. Flapper dresses, black bow ties, black jackets, white jackets, ballroom gowns. It is an exciting mixture of styles and eras.

She catches sight of the Professor heading over to her. He wears a formal evening suit with a top hat, white tie and tails. He sports a white carnation and has black and white dancing shoes.

"You look stunning," says the Professor.

"Thank you," replies Rachel. "And you look pretty good to."

"I thought I'd come in Fred Estaire style tonight. Show you a bit of my dancing," he smiles. "We're over by the white piano. We'll gather, then go for our Champagne at the dining table."

Charlotte wears a flamboyant "flappers" knee length dress, with frills and tasslled layers. It is light blue, turquoise and silver. She has beads and a band across her head with feather at the back. She comes through the crowd as Rachel approaches.

"Wow," says Rachel, "what an outfit."

"I wouldn't normally wear this but "Charlie boy" asked me to do it. Just for the performance. I'll be back in jeans after the clock strikes midnight. But until then I'll enjoy the frivolity of the headdress and the glamour of the boa."

"Let me introduce you," says the Professor.

Rachel instantly recognises the woman she saw kissing in the corridor.

"This is Rachel Foxe," says the Professor to the group.

"Oh, do you do the Foxtrot? Ha ha," asks Charles with an attractive, happy smile. Charlotte digs the young man in the chest with her elbow. He offers to shake Rachel's hand in appeasement and she takes it. He is handsome, with a strong nose and dark medium length hair, swept back into 1920's style. He wears a dinner suit with a black tie and red carnation. He has a quiet handsomeness. Not vain, not shouting about it.

"Don't mind him," says Charlotte. "It's his artistic temperament."

Rachel dwells on this, wanting to avoid meeting the Professor's fiancé, Barbara. She has a dark complexion and is pretty, with her hair cut into a 1920's style bob. Heavy, gold earings frame what looks like a surgically altered, stretched face with unnaturally full lips, hidden behind mascara and heavy red lipstick. Her tasselled dress is a purple version of Charlotte's but she has black heels and fishnet stockings. A black feather boa and beads drape around her shoulders. Her head band is golden with a black feather in the front. She languidly holds a long cigarette holder.

She looks like sugar and spice but it was obvious that you don't get what you see. The surface charm and sweetness underlay a subtle ruthlessness. She smiles and offers Rachel a gloved hand. "Charming to meet you."

"I love your feather boa," says Rachel trying to catch her gaze. Rachel wasn't sure if this was who Charlotte had referred to earlier as vampish. But the body language is clear.

Charlotte has folded her arms. "She's dressed to impress, as always, but I won't say, to kill."

Barbara closes her eyes, takes a moment and then turns to Charlotte. "To Kill A Mocking Bird. Ever read it?" She takes a fake puff on her fake cigarette and turns away.

Charles and Charlotte look at each other and shake their heads.

The Professor puts his arm around his fiancé and gathers them all together. "We are looked down upon by Triton, the messenger of the sea gods," announces the Professor. He looks at Rachel and continues, "shall we go "AND HEAR "OLD TRITON" BLOW HIS WREATHED HORN" and hear what Neptune and the mermaids have to say."

The Professor winks and Rachel knows that he is referring to Thomas.

They head towards the music that comes from a corridor to the left of the reception desk.

"Ah, Professor," says the assistant manager, "let me show you to your table," he is very helpful but when he notices Rachel at the back of the group he becomes sheepish as he leads them into the dining room.

⁓THE DINING ROOM⁓

The dining room follows the arc of the hotel. It is beginning to fill with diners and dancers, who take their places on stylish white plastic chairs at round tables. Their clothing reflects a strange mix of eras. At the far end is the dance area where a jazz band is playing. "I'm amazed that there are so many different styles of dress here," Rachel says.

"Well we've got the styles from two different eras, not only with the clothes but you'll also see it with the dancing, later," explains the Professor. "It's because the Wall Street Crash of 1929 brought a sudden end to the raging Jazz rhythms and the Charleston. The Swing Era followed on close behind with the Lindy Hop. But we prefer the 1920's Charleston style."

Rachel raises her eyebrows in appreciation of the explanation. Then as they head further into the room she looks to her right and notices a plaster relief that fills the wall.

"That's another Eric Gill," notes the Professor. "It's a map of North West England."

"It always turns peoples heads," jokes Charles, "its side on. North is to the left, south to the right."

Rachel tilts her head. "Ah yes, Blackpool Tower, and there's the Midland Hotel."

"Yes," explains the Professor, "and as this hotel was built by a Train company it shows a train on the North West coastline, from Whitehaven in the north to Birkenhead. My favourite part is The Lake District. I love this lady floating to meet her leaping lover, amongst the leafy trees and blue lakes. And look, hounds chasing a fox over rounded fells."

Rachel has little time to admire the scene over her shoulder as they are cajoled between the tables towards the far end of the room.

"It's a shame that there are tables everywhere," says Charles. "We could use the whole of this wooden floor. It'd be great for dancing."

Already at their table are two guests. There are place names but Rachel doesn't need to read Thomas's. She recognises him immediately, but pretends that he is completely unknown to her. She wonders at his motives as she looks around at all names to find her seat. It is next to Thomas's.

He stands to introduce himself. He is a thin man, with grey hair and a beard but he has a boyish look in his eyes and a charming smile. He wears a 1930's style pinstripe gangster double breasted suit with a black shirt and a white tie. He is still wearing his fedora hat. She sits at the meal table next to him.

Suzie is smiling through heavy red lipstick and mascara as she offers Rachel her hand across Thomas' lap. Although she is the same age as Barbara she looks younger because she is bubbly and enthusiastic. She has dark hair in a wave and wears a long, tight, red silk dress. "You look stunning. I think you'll have a great evening. And don't worry, Thomas will dance with you. Won't you Thomas."

Rachel notices how tightly Suzie clasps Thomas' leg. "What brings you here tonight?" Suzie continues.

Rachel sees the process of calculation going on underneath. But before she can reply...

"Suzie, darling," calls Barbara across the table.

"Oh, hello Barbara," says Suzie. "What a curiously charming headdress."

Barbara frowns, "I'll take that as a compliment," then puffs on her imaginary cigarette again.

"And you have a lovely necklace," adds Rachel to ease the tension.

"I agree, although I'm not normally interested in costume jewellery," says Suzie.

"Ah," exclaims the Professor. "Look what's on the menu." He whispers to Rachel, "they're old school friends," then begins to read out the menu, to ease the tension. "Iced melon or shrimps, cold soup, a main course of salmon or lamb followed by strawberries and ice cream and coffee - all served on the hotel's specially commissioned tableware."

The band begins to play another tune. "I love the High Class Jazz Band," says Thomas across the whole table. "They have such fire and inspiration." He turns to Suzie. "Let's have a quick dance before everyone arrives."

Suzie agrees and they both get up. He removes his hat and jacket to reveal a pin-striped waist-coat. As they move onto the floor he has a sprightly step. He wears spats and is so light on his feet he seems to be almost bouncing like a teenager. Suzie is thin and her long red, silk dress looks a little awkward to dance in. Either that or despite her slim frame she is slightly heavy and clumsy. She has to work at dancing, to make it look like it comes naturally.

Rachel enjoys watching the band more. The middle-aged men are all dressed in suits and wear black fedora hats.

The drums and the double bass set the cool beat as a red-hot Trumpet cries out, filling the room like a mighty sea horn, and is followed by the piping sound of a Clarinet. A piano flourish breaks the wall of sound and acts as an introduction to a Banjo solo.

"They've a great repertoire of classic jazz and swing," says Charles.

"And that's why they've got a growing following," adds the Professor.

"Yes, I like how light-hearted and entertaining they are," says Barbara. "Especially when they play comedy songs."

"But they are saving the best for later," says the Professor.

The song finishes and Suzie sits back down as Thomas glides over, offering Rachel a hand. She shakes her head.

"Why don't you get up and dance?" asks Suzie.

Rachel shakes her head again.

"Oh well. Thomas will dance with you later if you can't find anyone."

"That's very kind. I'm just happy to enjoy watching people dance at the moment. You both dance very well."

Suzie smiles her thanks for the compliment and then Rachel turns and continues. "Thomas, the Professor tells me that you work in antiques. I was reading about the work at the Midland. What do you think of it. Is it a restoration or a renovation?" Thomas holds a slightly bemused smile as he listens, almost mocking.

"Oh, I think that what they've done is marvellous," he says. "It gets the building used which is the main thing, but it is a conversion, not a restoration or a renovation."

"What do you mean?" asks Rachel.

"Well, if you have a piece of Art Deco furniture and add a glass cabinet to the top of it, one that was never there in the first place, then you wouldn't have restored it. You would've converted it."

"I still don't follow."

"Well," continues Thomas, "if you keep it the same as you find it, just stop it from getting worse, then its conservation. If you replace any damaged parts with old parts from other pieces of furniture then its restoration. If you replace all the old parts with completely new parts then its renovation. And if you add new bits that were never there in the first place then its conversion. So the bit that has been added to the top of the Midland makes it a conversion."

The Professor leans over the table. "Interesting. So, Thomas, what was that

Art Deco cabinet that you sold me? It's got a completely new door on it."

"Yes, that was half restoration, half renovation. These things aren't hard and fast. Anyway, it will still hold its value at auction."

The Professor laughs. "The Midland is a different case anyway. The new roof was part of the architect's original plan."

"Then it is a finishing of a construction," explains Thomas, "that still changes the historic building." He sits back, smiling.

Rachel is listening with interest. "Thank you for explaining that, it's really interesting." She is beginning to get a sense that Thomas is a jovial charmer. He is softly spoken but has a slightly frisky demeanour. "Anyway, how long have you been working in antiques here Thomas?"

"Oh, about ten years."

"And what were you doing before then?" asks Rachel.

"Oh, various things."

Rachel considers how Thomas is always ready with a smile and glows with a warm generosity of spirit. But, she reminds herself, that it doesn't mean that he is warm and generous. She decides to throw a stone in the pool and watch the ripples that it makes. "Well, either you just have one of those faces but I was sure I've seen you in London, maybe ten years ago."

Suzie splutters her water and then points across the room. "Oh, Lenny and Lindsey are here."

Rachel notices Charles and Charlotte straighten their backs and frown.

"Lenny's my ex," continues Suzie. "Thomas showed him how to teach the Lindy Hop."

Charlotte leans over and whispers to Rachel "Thomas encouraged Suzie to dance and then she got Lenny dancing to get him out of the way. They were our ex-students but they got their dancing "qualifications" and set themselves up as our "rivals", criticising our teaching to all our students. They take it far too seriously." They join the group and do the rounds of introductions.

Lindsey has dark hair tied back. She has a gaunt face and a hooked nose. Her piercing eyes narrow in judgment. She smiles. "Hi guys." Her rough voice sounds like she smoked for a number of years. She wears a yellow satin dress. It contrasts with her chilling forth rightness, that doesn't need to be spoken. She gets what she wants and won't let anyone stand in her way. Period. The smile is as false as a Cheshire cat. All is just business. Every action is calculated to an outcome.

Lenny stands behind her. He has a ginger moustache and is dressed for Lindy Hop. He wears a light brown v-neck tank-top over a white shirt. He takes off his cap and reveals his light coloured hair. It is close cropped at the sides and swept over from left to right. He has a strong frame and is quiet. Reaching over to Rachel he offers her a trembling hand that is sweaty to shake. It's as though he wants to be really nice but just doesn't know how to. The words don't quite come out, the gesture is hesitant, so Rachel can't tell what is under the surface.

Barbara rings her glass with a spoon, getting everyone's attention. "Now that we are all here let's have Champagne cocktails!" She attracts the attention of the assistant manager. "Waiter, can we have, Cognac, Angostura Bitters, a twist of lemon and some brown sugar lumps."

The assistant manager frowns but diligently heads out of the dining room.

The assistant manager quickly returns with the ingredients on a tray.

"It's my father's favourite," says Charlotte. "Dom Perignon, Vintage 2000. They always have a bottle of it."

The assistant manager picks up the bottle, rotates it and pops the cork.

"Ohh!"

"Enjoy," he says as he leaves them.

The Professor then pours the Champagne. "Mmm. A perfumed, inviting Champagne that is elegance personified."

Charlotte adds the cognac, which turns the drink amber.

Barbara adds the sugar lumps, which fizz in the bottom of the glass.

Lindsey says "no sugar lump for me, thank you."

"None at all for me," says Rachel.

"Oh come on, a tiny bit won't hurt," says Suzie.

"Oh no, I can't, I promised someone that I wouldn't."

"Here's to a splendid evening," says the Professor.

"Cheers." They all drink. Rachel has water.

"It floats on the palate with remarkable grace," says Suzie with an air of levity.

"Blending toasty aromas with freshly cut flowers," says Charles.

"with apricots and pears," says Charlotte

"And lingers with notes of mint and liquorice," finishes Lindsey.

≈THE DANCE≈

"What I don't understand," says Rachel, throwing it out to the whole table, "is what's the difference between the Charleston and the Lindy Hop?"

"Well," begins Charles, "the Charleston is a dance named after the city of Charleston in South Carolina. The rhythm began in African-American communities and was popularized in 1923 by a Broadway hit tune called The Charleston. The dance was considered quite immoral and is associated with young, white lady dancers, "flappers," and with the speakeasies, which sold illegal alcohol. It can be danced solo, with a partner or in groups of couples. The step starts off with a simple twist of the feet, then becomes fast, kicking the feet, forward and backward with a tap. Its danced to hot jazz and is different to the 1930s and 1940s Swinging Charleston which was adapted to swing jazz. But both take eight counts in the basic step. This Swinging Charleston integrated into Lindy Hop and became the Lindy Charleston. But it is all just "swing dance". Whether Lindy Hop, Lindy Charleston, West Coast Swing, East Coast Swing, Jive, Rock and Roll, Modern Jive. It's all just "swing"."

"Well, that's not really a proper explanation of Lindy," interrupts Lindsey. "The Lindy Hop evolved in Harlem, New York, in the late 1920s. It was called the Hop then changed after Charles Lindbergh did his "hop", flying across the Atlantic in 1927. In the 1930s the lindy-hoppers began to show off "air steps" - dramatic acrobatic moves, where both feet leave the ground, moves like the Hip to Hip, Side Flip, and Over the Back" she acts to suggest the motion of partnering an invisible woman in the air. "These steps are used in competition or performance, not in social dancing. The basic step for that is the swing-out."

Charles winces. "We'll show you a bit when we dance for our supper later."

"What do you mean?" asks Rachel.

"We are all doing a demonstration," explains Lindsey.

"But what would be really good," says Charles, "is if you get up and let us show you how to do the basic Charleston step."

Rachel is quick to reply. "I don't think my dress is designed for this kind of dancing."

Charles and Charlotte know that she's being coy. "Of course you can." They cajole her up and onto the dance floor, then stand either side of her.

"Swing the arm forward as the left leg steps forward with a bounce," says Charlotte.

Charles continues. "Then move back as the opposite arm and leg comes forwards. Your feet form a right angle with the leg at the ankle. That's good, but try extend your arms straight and put your hands at right angles."

The feet twisting is a little tricky but Rachel soon gets the hang of the basic steps and gets into the swing of things as she picks up the rhythm of the band.

"Good," says Charles. "But it's usually a heck of a lot faster. It's usually danced to high tempo music. Listen, we have to go, we're doing the couples dance off. We'll give you something more advanced after the group dance later."

Rachel thanks them both and they return to their table. Charles removes his jacket and puts it over his chair. He is wearing black braces revealing a hidden stylishness. Not over sophisticated, just a discrete, hidden elegance. A thoughtfulness in how everything is constructed. Rachel overhears him say to Charlotte, "Remember, it's not important, it's just dancing, don't let their aggression upset you."

Meanwhile Lindsey gets up, looking like the cat that will get the cream, although Lenny is not so sure. As they step onto the dance floor Rachel can see Lenny's flapping white trousers and his two tone brown shoes. He has all the right clothes in all the right order but they just don't sit together in a comfortable, elegant way. Style doesn't come naturally. He takes a partner hold with Lindsey on the dance floor. Her yellow dress is above knee high and fills out with a white undergarment.

She has white pumps and white socks but is clearly the one wearing the trousers.

"Are you not joining in Suzie? Thomas?" asks Rachel.

"Oh no," says Suzie, "we leave that to the others. It's far too stressful."

The dancing begins with the 1920s Charleston and the four dancers move forwards to the audience in an informal line. They perform 'strolls' and 'travelling' steps, taking the opportunity to "shine", interacting with the audience, employing comic walks and impersonations.

The couples then stand facing each other in a traditional closed partner dancing pose. The leader's right hand on the follower's back. The follower's left hand rests on the leader's shoulder. The leader's left hand and the follower's right hand clasp palm to palm, held at shoulder height, with their torsos touching.

The leaders touch their left foot behind them, but don't shift their weight, while the followers touch their right foot forward. Both bring their feet back together and then the leaders touch their right foot forward as the followers touch their left foot back.

Rachel watches and says to the Professor "I could do that."

Then the closed position is opened out so that both partners face forward.

"Jockey position," announces Thomas across the table.

The leaders step back onto their left foot, while the followers step back onto their right. They touch at their hips and have an arm touching each others' back, swinging their free arms as they would in solo Charleston.

"Side-by-side," announces Thomas again.

The followers then stand in front of the leaders and both step back onto their left feet, holding hands and arms swinging backwards and forwards.

"Tandem Charleston," announces Thomas, a final time.

The four dancers then contrast faster movements with slower, dragging steps. They create variations on the familiar dance steps, responding to the music, expressing themselves in improvised choreographies.

"I couldn't do that," says Rachel.

Then the music changes and the couples begin to dance the Lindy Hop.

All comes alive, with the frills of Charlotte's turquoise dress spinning along with her and with the yellow of Lindsey's dress dazzling the eye as she turns over Lenny's back.

"I wouldn't do that if you paid me," says Rachel.

As they dance the Professor whispers to Rachel. "It's hard to decide if Lindsey has had surgery or not. There was never any expression in that face in the first place. There is no warmth in her. She seems to be waiting until the opportunity arises for her to pounce, and no opportunity is missed."

"Oh, I hope Lenny doesn't drop her," says Rachel as she sees her held upside down, "I can't bear to watch."

"Oh don't worry about her," the Professor replies. "She's the opposite of China. Simply unbreakable, but willing to break all around if she doesn't get her way. Destroys it, and then moves onto the next thing."

Charles and Charlotte are clearly the better dancers, their showy and physically impressive "stunt" moves steal the show and the audience responds with cheers and applauds.

After the "dance off" the band stops playing and their leader, the trumpet player, announces "Lets give another round of applause for our dance teachers, Charles and Charlotte, and Lenny and Lindsey. Enjoy your meal and we'll return later, to bring you more music to dance to."

The audience applauds and the dancers return, red-faced and exhausted, to their seats.

❧THE MEAL☙

The meal follows a traditional Midland Hotel menu from the 1930's. Iced melon, shrimps, cold soup, salmon, lamb, strawberries, ice cream and finally coffee.

As the coffee is poured Lenny, Suzie and Thomas excuse themselves from the table. Rachel drinks her coffee and then excuses herself as well.

On her way to the toilets she sees Lenny and Suzie in the corridor. She is against the wall and he is standing over her, his arms either side. They haven't seen Rachel as she overhears Lenny. "We're in this together."

Suzie shakes her head, then notices Rachel. "Lenny was just looking for something he lost, a long time ago." She smiles and breaks away from his arms.

She straightens her dress and heads towards the hotel lobby.

When Rachel returns to her seat, after her visit to the toilet, she looks at the reflection of the dining room, in the tall glass of the sun lounge windows. Then she notices a movement beyond it. It is two figures. She can just make out that it is Thomas and Suzie. He holds her arms but she struggles free. She tries to swallow something and it looks like he taking a bottle of tablets from her. She storms off.

As Rachel is wondering what was going on they both return to the table, as if nothing has happened.

"Okay everyone, its time for the group dance," announces Charles. He arranges the dancers into a loose circle on the dance floor. They all begin to dance and then form two long lines, facing each other. They follow steps "called" by

Charles. "Full Turn Round." This is then done by everyone in turn.

The group perform the same step until a new step is "called" by Lenny. "Hop on the left and half turn round." The dancers hop on the left foot across to the other side of the floor, turning 180 degrees to the left.

The group then splinters and people begin to free dance, improvising to the music or copying dancers around them. They dance alone or partner, men with women, or women together.

The Charleston dancers gather with Charles and Charlotte and Lindy Hoppers gather with Lenny and Lindsey.

As the teachers dance a circle of dancers forms around them. Rachel wants to watch. She gets up and tries to see over the crowds. "What's going on?" she asks.

"I think they're doing the "Jitterbug"," a man in a white suit replies.

Rachel looks confused.

"Yeah, so called 'cause they look like a bunch of "jitterbugs" on the dance floor, bouncing around."

But as they both get closer, to see the dancers, something is clearly wrong. Charles and Charlotte are writhing around on the dance-floor.

Rachel holds a hand over her mouth and runs back to the table. But everyone there is collapsed on the floor, bent double in pain.

The room fills with screams and only the assistant manager saves the situation, announcing on the band's microphone. "Please stay calm. Can all guests please make their way quietly to the lobby area. If there are any doctors or First Aiders please stay here to help. Everyone else, please make your way back to the lobby."

☙THE SUNLOUNGE☙

The sick guests are helped through a side door to the sun-lounge. They are finding it difficult to breathe so the double doors and windows facing the sea are opened to let in some air.

The tall glass windows stretch for the full length of the hotel. But there is no view, just the reflection of light back into the hotel. The victims sit hunched over the black leather chairs. They stare, from gaunt faces, at the floor. They have pains in the stomach.

Lenny hangs onto one of the white poles that supports the roof. He clutches his stomach, massaging it. Barbara rushes outside to be sick.

The waitresses bring them blankets and put water and tea onto the glass tables.

They have headaches and are lightheaded.

As the air becomes cold the doors are closed.

Slowly they begin to recover but the Professor gets worse.

He is rushed to hospital but before he can get there he dies.

When Charlotte is told she cries out into the night. She is inconsolable about the loss of her father.

All is dark.

⁕THE INVESTIGATION⁕

Everyone sits, drinking tea, recovering.

Charles is consoling Charlotte when Lindsey calls out. "I think it's Charles who has done this. He pretends to be "oh so nice" but it makes me sick. He's been so nasty to us. I know what he's capable of."

"I can't believe you have the audacity to suggest that," reels Charles, in shock at the suggestion. "Despite all you've done we've been nothing but courteous to you."

"And Charles's art work is dubious," adds Lenny, "it's all about sex and death and pain. He probably wants Charlotte's inheritance money so he can go down to London and set up a gallery and sell his art."

"What do you know about anything," fumes Charles. "Yes, no one around here appreciates my artwork and I want to leave the area, to go back down to London, to put on exhibitions. I make no secret of the fact, but I'd never kill to do it. And just because I paint in the style of the 1920's Surrealists doesn't mean I'm a murderer."

"Look," says Rachel, "all we know is that it appears the Champagne cocktails were poisoned."

But as Rachel is speaking the assistant manager returns with the receptionist. "We've finished looking in your rooms."

Everyone looks, expectant of some evidence.

"A bottle of Dom Perignon, Vintage 2000, has been found in Charles and Charlotte's room."

"So I have a bottle of the same champagne in my room," says Charles. "It's Charlotte's favourite. In fact it was Charlotte who got her father drinking the stuff in the first place and her father gave that bottle to me for us to share."

"The evidence is there Charles," says Lenny, "stop trying to deny it."

Charlotte stops crying, "Lenny, you just want to frame Charles…"

"Why would he want to do that?" demands Lindsey.

"You've been telling everyone that our lessons are too easy," says Charlotte, "that we don't teach right, that our music is no good. Always trying to poach the people we spent years putting lots of care into teaching. When that didn't work you started saying all sorts about us, waiting for us to stoop to your level and insult you back. So that you can tell everyone how horrid we are. And now you've begun to believe the lies that you've been telling everyone about us. All because you've wanted to take over what took us years to build up. And now you've ruined what was once a very pleasant scene."

As Charlotte delivers her reply Rachel looks at the Champagne bottle on the table, then she examines the cork. "It's a bit hard to see this without my glasses, however, it looks like the cork has a needle hole that could have been used for injecting poison. The hole has been filled with what looks like glue." Rachel takes the cork over to the new bottle. "And it looks like the bottle from your room has the same marks on the cork's wrapper."

"That's an interesting turn of events," says the assistant manager. "Because we also found a syringe, in Lindsey's room."

"I'm diabetic. I need to use a syringe or I would die." Lindsey's casts her eyes down and then looks at Charles. "Look, I'm sorry, I shouldn't jump to conclusions, accusing you."

"Exactly. How do you think we feel?" asks Charles. "You know, someone could have given that champagne to the Professor, to pass on to us, to kill us!"

"So, who else could have a syringe," splutters Charlotte.

"I don't mean to get anyone into trouble here, only, Suzie asked me for a syringe," says Lindsey. "I gave it her, but had no idea what it was for."

"I know why," cries Charlotte, her eyes red. "Thomas is already married and Suzie didn't want anyone to find out. My father found out when he overheard Thomas on his phone to Suzie one night, here in the cocktail bar, saying that he thought his ex-wife was getting wind of where he was and wanted a divorce, he said that he would rather see her dead. And that's why Rachel's here, to investigate all about Thomas. And Suzie wanted my father out of the way before he could tell anyone."

"So this could be the motive," says Rachel, "To get rid of the Professor so that no one would learn that your beloved Thomas' real name is Cedric Johnson and that he is already married. That he's a bigamist."

Thomas' face goes white. His cheeky demeanour falls away. "Well deducted," says Thomas.

"Well deduced," replies Rachel.

Thomas just shakes his head. "I won't go back to her."

"She doesn't want you back. She just wants the evidence for a full divorce, and wants you to sign the papers."

"She'll get nothing, and I didn't kill no one!"

"No, I don't believe you did, still," continues Rachel, "you're likely to be in prison for bigamy and the rest."

Suzie is now sobbing. She grabs her pills from Thomas' jacket and swallows a handful.

"They aren't going to help," says Rachel, "you are still the main suspect."

"Ha, that's ridiculous," snorts Suzie. "If you must know, I gave the syringe to Barbara. She asked me for it. Although, I didn't know why she wanted one at the time."

"Rubbish Suzie!" replies Barbara. "It's nothing to do with me!"

Suzie laughs again. "Even when we were friends at school you used to try to weadle your way out of things and put the blame on me."

"But Suzie," says Rachel. "I saw Thomas taking some tablets off you in the sun lounge, earlier in the evening."

"She was upset," interrupts Thomas, "because Lenny was giving her problems. I told her not to get hysterical. And not to take any more of these." He reaches into his pocket and gets out a small bottle of pills. "They are anti-depressants. You don't know the stress she's under at the moment, from work and from Lenny."

Lenny shakes his head.

"Is that true Lenny? Is this what I saw you arguing with Suzie about earlier? Saying that you were "in this together". Is that what it was all about?"

Lenny hangs his head in shame. "Yes. I just want her back. That's all. I still love her. I always will. But I would never threaten her, or anything."

Lindsey looks away from him. Her pride dented more than her heart hurt. Lenny was useful. That was all.

Between sobs Charlotte manages to continue. "But there is more that my father said. He'd been disgusted to hear what Thomas was saying so he went down to the cocktail bar toilets. He heard Thomas and the assistant manager of the Midland talking. Saying that they had been working on a plan to steal the Eric Gill frieze on the way back from exhibition or something. My father came out and confronted them, warning them not to plan any further or that he would tell the police."

"That's complete rubbish," says the assistant manager, "and I consider what you just said to be slander."

"Well, it's very interesting circumstantial evidence," says Rachel. "But let's not get sidetracked from the main case. I think that Suzie remains the main suspect. After all, Suzie has a motive, she wanted the Professor out of the way, and she was given a syringe."

"Yes, which I gave to Barbara," snorts Suzie in retort.

～THE EVIDENCE～

At that moment a young man in glasses puts his head around the doors to the sun lounge.

"Excuse me," he says.

Everyone turns to face him.

"It's so tragic. Professor Bill was an absolute genius in the field of Toxicology. Well respected and loved by everyone."

"And you are?" asks Rachel.

"I'm Simon Gibson," says the young man. "I'm sorry - I was, one of the Professor's PhD students. Last week, in the laboratory, the Professor told me how he needed to restock on arsenic because some had gone missing. He said he couldn't work out where such a large amount had gone. Enough to kill an elephant. He was going to call the police but asked me to look into it first. I've come straight from the lab tonight, so I've got my bag with me. I can do a toxicology test if you like."

Rachel agrees and the young man tests the glasses, the bottles and the sugar lumps.

"The only thing I found is that there is arsenic in the Champagne bottle and each of the glasses, only there is more arsenic in the glass of the Professor. It's arsenic trioxide, which is 500 times more toxic than pure arsenic. He died of arsenicosis, chronic arsenic poisoning. The first symptoms are involuntary muscular dysfunction, vomiting, abdominal pains and diarrhoea. I don't really want to describe the Professor's end, but I'm sure that they made it as comfortable for him as possible."

He looks at the forlorn dancers. "Don't worry, they will do tests on all of you to determine if you've been poisoned by the same compound. If this is the case then sub-lethal doses can lead to cardiovascular problems, liver and kidney problems and abnormalities in your blood. You may even suffer hair loss."

Charlotte is inconsolable in Charles's arms.

"So, we have the motive," says Rachel, "we just don't have the clues, yet. And its puzzling me how there was more poison in the Professor's glass than in any of the others. So, lets look a little closer at the cork. It looks like the arsenic was injected through the cork. Maybe the syringe was emptied into the bottle, the needle kept in, then glue injected into the cork as the needle was withdrawn from the hole. This fast setting glue then hardened, stopping the air from escaping and the pressure being lost."

Rachel looks at everyone's face. They are in varying degrees of discomfort and grief. The ladies' have mascara mixed with tears smudged around their eyes. It's understandable that some people are more upset than others but she is perplexed as she sits in front of Barbara.

"Barbara," says Rachel. "You seem to be very stoical about the loss of your fiancé. A little too stoical in my opinion."

"I can't feel what I should be feeling," replies Barbara. "I'm so ashamed. Maybe I never really loved him. I don't know. But I would never have harmed a hair on his head."

"You knew the Professor liked champagne cocktails," presses Rachel.

Charlotte stares at her. "I've been suspicious of you for a long time."

"But who delivered the champagne," asks Rachel, rhetorically. "It was the assistant manager." She turns to face him. "So you are in on this as well?"

"Yes, I made sure that particular vintage bottle was available. I put the champagne in the kitchen. It was given to me by Barbara. But I had no idea it was poisoned."

"So why have you been covering for her right until now?" asks Charles.

"Barbara and the hotel assistant manager are lovers," explains Rachel. "She wanted to get rid of the Professor and gain his inheritance and he was just interested in the money. That's why he wanted to steal the Eric Gill frieze."

"Like I said. That's complete rubbish," says Sebastian.

"And I don't see what you think could possibly be my motive in all of this," says Barbara.

"My father was very wealthy," says Charlotte, "and you guessed that he wanted to break off his engagement to you. So you wanted to get your share of the inheritance before he changed his will."

"So because he was a Professor of Toxicology," explains Rachel, "you could easily steal poison from him. You wanted to see your fiancé dead before he could change his will."

"However, you didn't know my father had already changed it, did you! He had misgivings about you and wanted to call the wedding off. And he suspected something was wrong long before that, so he changed his will!"

Barbara's face is frozen, her brain working overtime. "Actually, I knew I was out of the will. Your father told me. So I had no motive to do it."

"You just made that up," replies Charlotte.

"No, it's true."

"So why wouldn't you look at anyone when you said that?" asked Rachel

The fiancé's demeanour changes. "But it's true." She reaches for her handkerchief to dab a fake tear but as she does so a small plastic bag falls from her purse. Rachel quickly picks up the bag and finds that it has traces of brown sugar in it. "Mmm. Big enough for one sugar lump. This may be just the clue we need."

"You gave everyone a low dose to cover your tracks," she continues, "but one of the Champagne cocktails had extra poison. You put the sugar cubes in the cocktails. But Simon found that there was no arsenic in the sugar cubes from the table. Why, because you put a poisoned sugar lump, from this little bag, into the

Professor's drink, and then tried to frame Charles and Charlotte with another, identical, poisoned Champagne bottle!"

Barbara tries to grab the bag. Charles grabs her hand and Rachel observes that the polish on the fiancé's nails looked a little bit rough. "And you've got glue on your finger nails.

Rachel hands the bag to Simon as Barbara's face seems to crack. "It was Suzie! She said I should inject arsenic into a bottle of his favourite Champagne. She wanted me to get rid of him and Charlotte in one go."

"Rubbish!" cries Suzie.

"Suzie," spits Barbara, "you were infatuated with Charles and had wanted to take over from Charlotte. You wanted to see Charles destroyed when he was not interested in you. And when you met Thomas, who could teach a bit of dancing, you got Thomas to help Lenny set up classes to destroy Charles's business and that got Lenny nicely out of the way in the process."

"You found Thomas' antiques business exciting and lucrative," says Rachel, "and were in on the plan with the assistant manager to steal the Eric Gill. When Thomas told you that the Professor knew about the plan and that he was already married it tipped you over the edge. You didn't want anyone to know. So you needed to get rid of him and you got your childhood friend, the one you had always controlled, Barbara, the Professor's fiancé, to steal poison from the Professor's study."

"I honestly didn't think she'd do it," says Suzie, straight faced. "I'll never forgive myself."

"It is God who forgives," says Rachel. "You knew full well she would do what you suggested. I think you will find that you are a conspirator to the murder."

Suzie's face turns as sour as Angostura bitters.

It is now Suzie who cries out into the night.

All is dark.

~EPILOGUE~

Rachel is in London, looking from her window, over the garden at the back of the Business Design Centre. She strokes Troubles.

"I don't know about you, but this has been absolutely draining."

The cat purrs.

"Well, arsenic was found in the plastic bag and that confirmed all our suspicions. I'll never understand what make people capable of doing these things. Perhaps they just can't help hurting the innocent. Oh Troubles," Rachel sighs, "If only everyone was as unquestionably loyal as you."

The cat nestles his head into her lap.

"What was that quote? "THERE IS GOOD HOPE THAT THOU MAYEST SEE THY FRIENDS"."

She strokes the cat then puts him down and picks up the phone.

"Hello Gwen. This is Rachel Foxe. I don't know where to begin, but it's not good. I'm afraid I have some very sad news…"

☙☠❧